First Little Readers™

Gary the Monster

by Liza Charlesworth

ISBN: 978-1-338-29790-4

Illustrated by Tammie Lyon

First printing, June 2018.

 Published by Scholastic Inc. Printed in Jiaxing, China.

This is Gary.

Gary is big.
Gary is green.
Gary is hairy.

And Gary thinks EVERYTHING
is scary.

He sees a black cat
and runs away.
"That cat is so scary!"
screams Gary.

He sees an old house
and runs away.
"That house is so scary!"
screams Gary.

He sees a flying bat
and runs away.
"That bat is so scary!"
screams Gary.

He sees a tall scarecrow
and runs away.
"That scarecrow is so scary!"
screams Gary.

Gary runs down to the lake.
He hides behind a tree.

Then he looks in the water.
Guess what he sees?

It is big.
It is green.
It is hairy.

"That monster is so, so,
so, so scary!"
screams Gary.

An owl in the tree
begins to laugh,
"Gary, that monster is you!"

Wow!
The owl is right.
That monster IS Gary!

Gary feels silly.
"From now on,
I will be brave," he says.

Then a huge fish jumps
out of the lake.